STEPS TO READING

Dear Parent:

Congratulations! Your child is taking the first steps on an exciting journey. **The destination? Independent reading!**

STEPS TO READING will help your child get there. The programme offers three steps to reading success. Each step includes fun stories and colourful art, and the result is a complete literacy programme with something for every child.

Learning to Read, Step by Step!

(1) **Start to Read   Nursery – Preschool**
• **big type and easy words** • **rhyme and rhythm** • **picture clues**
For children who know the alphabet and are eager to begin reading.

(2) **Let's read together   Preschool – Year 1**
• **basic vocabulary** • **short sentences** • **simple stories**
For children who recognise familiar words and sound out new words with help.

(3) **I can read by myself   Years 1-3**
• **engaging characters** • **easy-to-follow plots** • **popular topics**
For children who are ready to read on their own.

STEPS TO READING is designed to give every child a successful reading experience. The year levels are only guides. Children can progress through the steps at their own speed, developing confidence in their reading, no matter what their year.

Remember, a lifetime love of reading starts with a single step!

By Apple Jordan
Illustrated by Alex Maher

This edition published by Parragon in 2011

Parragon
Queen Street House
4 Queen Street
Bath BA1 1HE, UK

ISBN 978-1-4454-2114-8

Printed in Malaysia

DISNEY · PIXAR

TOY STORY

Buzz's Backpack Adventure

PaRragon

Bath · New York · Singapore · Hong Kong · Cologne · Delhi
Melbourne · Amsterdam · Johannesburg · Auckland · Shenzhen

Andy could not wait for school. Today was space day!

"I will bring my space ranger, Buzz Lightyear," he said.

Buzz was excited.
He loved
space day!

In class,
Andy learned
about space.

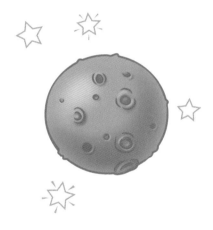

He learned
about the
stars and the
moon.

He learned
about the
sun and the
planets.

Brring!

The bell rang.

Lunchtime!

Buzz hopped out
of Andy's backpack.
He was ready
for fun!

Buzz saw the stars
and the moon.
He saw the planets.

Buzz could not
wait to explore.

Buzz saw
a hamster.
"Greetings,
strange creature,"
he said.

Buzz lifted the lid
to get a closer
look.

13

Uh-oh!
The hamster
jumped out.
It ran off.

"Come back!"

Buzz cried.

"I mean you no harm."

Oops!
Buzz fell into
a jar of paint.

"Blast!" cried Buzz.
"I must clean
up and find
that creature."

Buzz looked for
the hamster
inside a desk.

Buzz saw old gum
and chewed pencils,
but no hamster.

Then Buzz met
some clay aliens.
He thought they
were space toys.

"Greetings,"
he said.
"Have you seen a
furry creature?"

They did not answer.
Buzz shook hands
with a space toy.
Its arm fell off.

"Sorry about that!"
Buzz cried.
He ran away.

Buzz landed on
a tower made
of blocks.

It wobbled

back and forth.

Crash!

At last it came

toppling down.

"Oh, no!" said Buzz.
"I must clean up
this big mess!"

"All done!" said Buzz.
Then the bell rang.
The class came
back from lunch.

Buzz hopped
into Andy's backpack.
No one saw him.

The class got ready
for show-and-tell.
Andy went first.

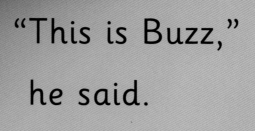

"This is Buzz,"
he said.
"Buzz is the BEST
space ranger ever!"

31

Now turn
over for the
next story...

By Kitty Richards

Disney · PIXAR

The Great Toy Escape

Bath · New York · Singapore · Hong Kong · Cologne · Delhi
Melbourne · Amsterdam · Johannesburg · Auckland · Shenzhen

Andy's toys love
to play.
But Andy is grown up.
He does not play
with his toys
anymore.

The toys must find
a new home.
They climb
into a car.

The car goes

to Sunnyside Daycare.

Sunnyside is full of toys!

A bear named Lotso is
in charge.

There are kids
at Sunnyside every day.
Andy's toys are happy.
The kids will play
with them!

But Woody is not happy.

He misses Andy.

He leaves.

It is time to play!

The little kids pull.

They throw.

They yell.

The toys do not like it.

The toys want
to go home.
But the door is locked!

Lotso is mean.

He will not let

Andy's toys leave.

Lotso and his gang lock
up Andy's toys!

Then Woody comes back.

He has a plan.

They will escape!

That night,
Woody and Slinky
steal the key!

The toys sneak outside.
They do not
make a sound.

The toys try to escape.

Oh, no!

They fall

into a garbage truck.

The truck goes
to the dump.
The toys are
in danger!
They must escape.

They run!
Woody tells them
to hurry.
They look
for a way out.

They slide!
The toys hold hands
to stay together.

At last,

they escape!

The toys hide
in the garbage.
They go back
to Andy's house.

The toys are safe.

They are happy

to be home.

Andy finds his toys
a new owner.
She loves to play!
And the toys love
their new home.